TO TESS

First published in hardback in Great Britain by Digital Leaf in 2014

ISBN: 978-1-909428-05-8

Text copyright © James Thorp 2014. Illustrations copyright © Angus Mackinnon 2014
The author and illustrator assert the moral right to be identified as the author and illustrator of the work.

digitalleaf

SUPERHAIRiES

PRESENT

Dog On Stills

~JAMES THORP & ANGUS MACKINNON~

This world is filled with wonderful dogs
of every shape and colour,
from small and white to purple and tall
not one looks like the other.

'So brilliant they are,' thought Medium Dog,
'that nobody notices me.
With my everyday hair and my medium shape
what more in this world could I be?'

With a sigh and a frown and a scratch of the head
Mr Medium Dog went to hide in his shed
where he banged and he crashed for a night and a day
though what he was building, no one could say.

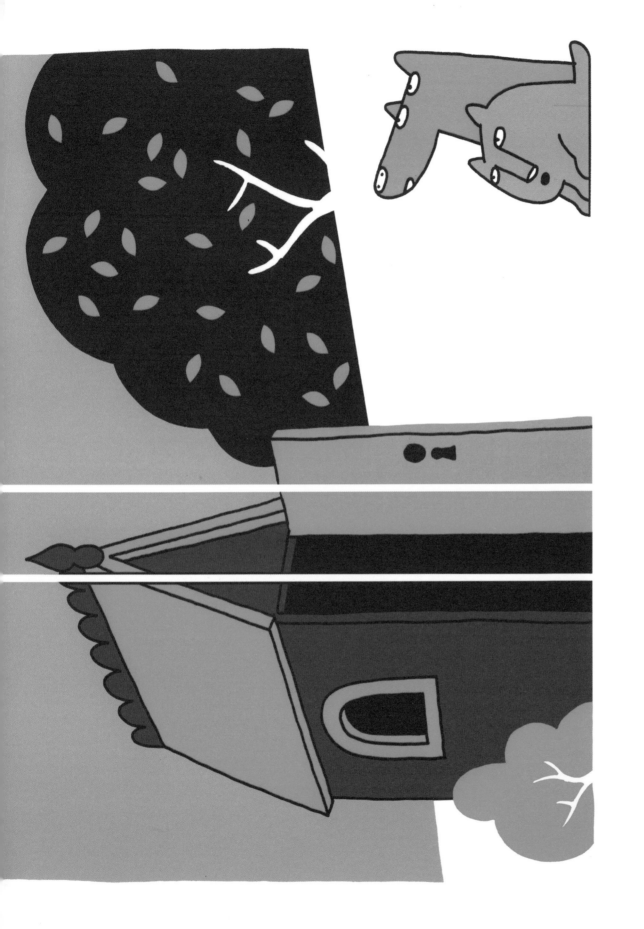

Early next morning his friends heard a bark
and filled with excitement they ran to the park
where on wobbly stilts with a smile in his eye
they saw Medium Dog waving down from the sky.

'Hold on - not so fast,' shouted Millie and Ron
but nothing could stop their old friend, he was gone.
They ran through the bushes and called out his name
but each time he answered, he answered the same:

'I once was an everyday medium hound
with my tail in the air and my nose to the ground

but now I'm as tall as a towering tree
and all of the creatures take notice of me.

On one leg, with no hands, he danced in the sun
as dancing on stilts is most excellent fun.

He whistled down chimneys...

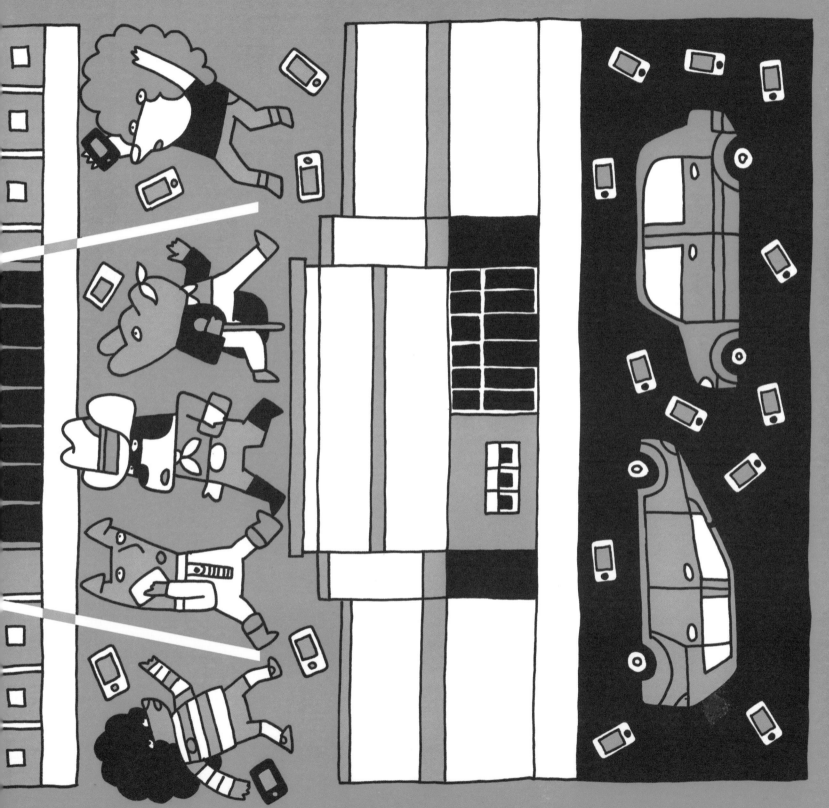

'There's nothing I like more than fooling around.'

High in the branches, far from his home
Medium Dog found himself quite alone.
He chased after squirrels to join them in play
but they called him 'a monster' and scurried away.

'I don't think I like being wonderful now',
said Medium Dog, staring hungrily down
at the bowlful of biscuits just under his feet,
'what a wonderful treat, only quite out of reach.'

'If you want to have dinner,' said Millie and Ron,
'then listen up old friend and follow along
there's a forest of fruit that lies up in these hills
that can only be reached by a dog who wears stilts.'

So Medium Dog, with a growl and a sneeze
ran up to the forest to hide in the trees
where he munched and he crunched and he gulped and he gobbled
filling his belly until it all wobbled.

And just as he thought that the fruits had been eaten
and he was the dog that could never be beaten
a single pink apple popped out on the tree
that was bigger and brighter and taller than he.

'I must have that apple,' said Dog with a swipe
of the hand as his belly swung left and then right
and his stilts started shaking as taking a leap...

...he fell to the earth in a tumbling heap.

Next thing he knew he was safe home in bed
with a bruise on his bum and a lump on his head.
His friends Ron and Millie were close by his side
and when he awoke they excitedly cried:

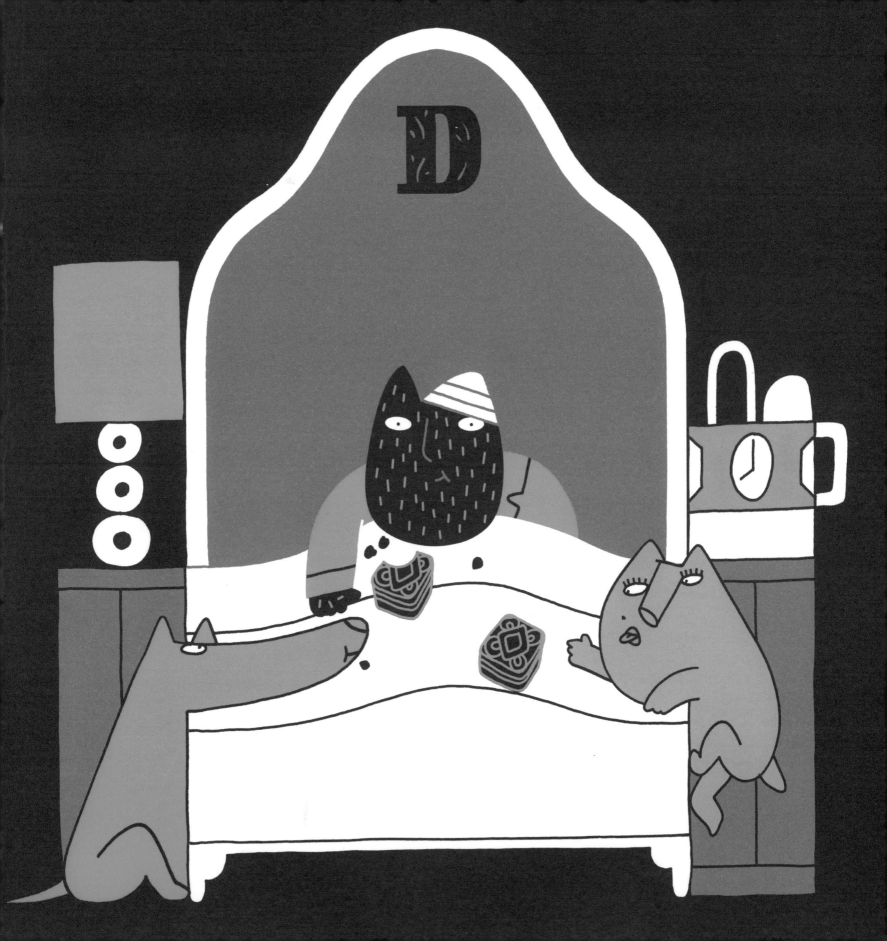

'A tall dog
a small dog
a square dog or blue,
a brown dog
or round dog
an old one or new,
as flat as a pancake
or high as a star,
we think you're dog-wonderful
just as you are.'

Medium Dog thanked his friends with a smile
and scratching his head said, 'I'll sleep for a while',
but as soon as the lights in his room had gone out...

The End

DOG ON STILTS
THE MUSICAL
LISTEN ALONG AT SUPERHAIRIES.COM/DOGONSTILTS

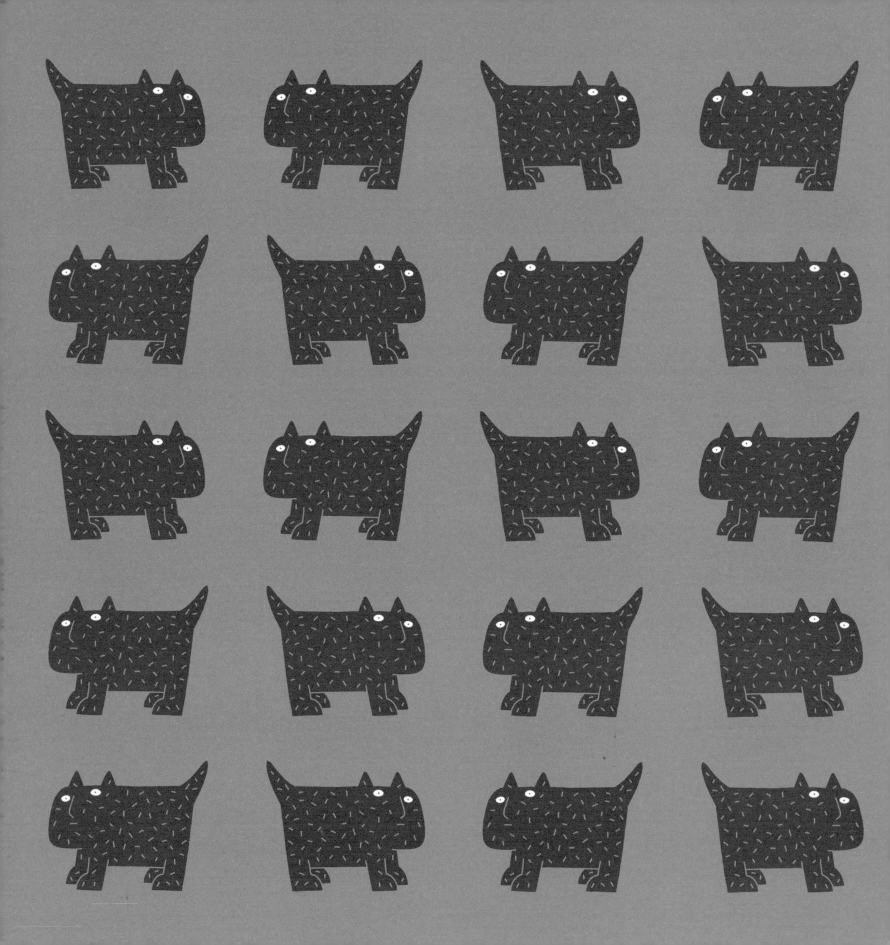